I0556077

So Pucking Wrong

Wrong

Thin Ice #9

Charity Parkerson

Punk & Sissy Publications

Copyright

—Warning: This book is intended for readers over the age of 18. Some of my books contain allusions to past abuse and trauma.

CONTENTS

Introduction

*LIFE IS ALWAYS A **game to Harlan. His time with Tanner is no different. Until it is.***

Harlan is living his best life. Ten years with a professional football team has him rolling in dough and all the fun times with whoever he wants. Things have gotten a bit weird the past year. It started with a trip to Canada for a birthday party. A chance meeting with the owner of a pro hockey team has him messed up. The silver fox—who is more like a bear—won't get out of his head, or stop showing up around every corner. Harlan doesn't know what to do about this new-found distraction.

Not one time in Tanner's life has he not gotten what he wants. That's just how it is. There's nothing or no one he can't buy. He wishes he could say Harlan was no different. Unfortunately, the guy can't be caught. He's young, cocky, famous, and rich. For once, Tanner has nothing to offer except a near twenty-year age difference and an inconveniently long-distance relationship. That's not stopping Tanner. He knows there's a way to own Harlan. He has one plan. It will either backfire spectacularly or win him the love of a lifetime.

So Pucking Wrong is the ninth book Charity Parkerson's Thin Ice series. These books are steamy sports romances meant to heat up your day. This series is best enjoyed when read in order.

CHAPTER ONE

As HARD AS HARLAN tried to focus on the action taking place on the ice, he couldn't. His gaze kept sliding from the owner's box window to the man whose laughter captivated the room. Tanner Paige was fifty-one. He had dark blond hair that was more gray than anything. His dark blue eyes always swam with happiness. The lines around his eyes proved he smiled more often than not. His bear-sized body was nothing compared to his monster-sized personality. He laughed like a man who knew his worth, which was somewhere in the billions. In fact, this was Tanner's box. He owned the New Orleans' Chuckers. The ice was his. The building was his. Every eye in the room was his, including Harlan. But Harlan would be damned if he gave Tanner the satisfaction of knowing it. Tanner already had too much at his fingertips. Thankfully, that was true of Harlan too.

Ten years ago, straight out of college, Harlan had entered the draft. He had been picked up by Los Angeles and that had been his team, his family, and his home ever since. He was by no means the highest paid kicker in the league, but he was definitely valued. His record spoke volumes and his pay matched. It was a good life. One that didn't need the complication known as Tanner Paige.

Another loud laugh filled the air, turning Harlan's head. Tanner stood with Harlan's brothers and brothers-in-law, all of which lived in New Orleans now. He was the only brother who still lived too far away to visit often. With both his brothers now happily married, and working on their relationship with him, Harlan felt obligated to try too. He loved his brothers. Always had. Maybe he felt a little closer to his younger brother, Matt, than he did his older brother, Rider. That was mostly because Rider had moved out when Harlan was nine. Matt was only five years younger. They'd had more time together. Plus, Rider had always been more like a third parent. That made things odd between them. More lecturing and less brotherly love.

Still, as Harlan watched Rider smile and chat with Matt's husband, he wished he didn't feel like the odd man out all the time. He recognized that was mostly due to him living far away. Unfortunately, it also had a great deal to do with him not being anything like them. Rider was a brooder, but steady. Matt was a worrier, but also equally steady. Harlan chose freedom from responsibility. He breathed easier while not giving a fuck. Rider and Matt had spent years in misery due to their narcissistic mother. Harlan hadn't because he didn't give a shit and she knew it. Middle child syndrome. No one noticed him and he flipped two birds to family ties. The situation seemed to work for everyone. Except sometimes, like now, he felt a little too much like an outsider. He had to go back to watching the game.

A swarm of skates and jerseys moved across the ice. Harlan didn't truly see a thing. Since Rider managed the Chuckers and Tanner owned them, he supposed that was who he hoped would win. Otherwise, he had no skin in the game. They were up by one with seconds left. All they had to do was hold them. Harlan focused hard and tried to care. The game was the safest place for his mind.

"How long will you be in town?"

Harlan was trying so hard not to notice his family, he nearly jumped out of skin at Matt's husband's question. He tried to hide his reaction as he looked Slater's way. Harlan pasted on a carefree smile.

"I'm not sure yet. The season just ended, so...?" He shrugged.

The buzzer sounded, signaling the end of the game. They glanced toward the window. The Chuckers had won. Everyone cheered while Harlan returned to his conversation with Slater.

"Matt would love for you to come by for a visit while you're here. He misses you quite a bit."

Honestly, that surprised Harlan. Matt had recently cut the family from his life for nearly a year. Then out of blue, Harlan had received an invitation to Matt's wedding... to a duke, of all things. It was a little strange to be related to royalty, especially since Slater—while obviously polished—was so normal. He was just some guy with a nice accent and an expensive suit. Harlan saw what Matt saw in him. Plus, the guy openly adored Matt in every way. That was a hard trait to resist.

Matt materialized at Slater's side.

Slater immediately tucked him close.

The move was so obviously natural for them. Matt just moved into place without ever looking away from Harlan. He was all smiles. "Hey. You've been standing here all by yourself all night. I haven't gotten to talk to you at all."

Harlan laughed. "It was easier than trying to get a word in with Tanner here."

Matt snorted. "Yeah. He is very much the center of attention everywhere he goes."

Slater nodded. "He's always been that way. Larger than life."

The comment caught Harlan off guard. "Have you known Tanner long?"

"My family helped him with a tax situation several years ago. He's damnably hard to dislike. My mother is very smitten. They've stayed in touch."

A bark of laughter burst from Harlan. "Ours too. They met at a surprise party Tanner threw for Rider. Our mom took one look at him and saw her second husband. Thankfully, Tanner is wise to her ways and avoids her as much as possible."

Matt's eyebrows rose. "You're joking."

"That's right. I forgot you missed that party." Harlan chuckled. "You really missed a show. Mom was on her A game."

"Oh, my god." Matt sounded rightfully horrified. There was nothing their mom loved more than money. That included her kids. Some people just weren't cut out to be parents.

Rider and Ben joined the conversation. "What did we miss?"

Harlan laughed at Rider's husband's question. "We were talking about Mom at Rider's birthday party."

Rider groaned. "You've never seen so much cleavage-fluffing in your life."

Everyone laughed.

A weight lifted from Harlan's shoulders.

"People are laughing without me. Don't leave me out." Tanner was all smiles as he joined them.

They tried hard not to look at each other. Thankfully, Rider had things under control. "We were poking fun at your shoes."

The loud laugh that burst from Tanner made Harlan smile. He couldn't help it. Tanner was like happiness in a bottle. It was contagious.

Tanner lifted his foot, showing off a pair of gaudy sneakers with the team's logo plastered all over them. "They're my good luck shoes, and you see they work. We won, didn't we?"

"I'm pretty sure that was Medvedkov's doing."

Tanner chuckled at Ben's response. "Maybe a little of that too." Tanner, being the center of attention, gave Harlan a free pass to stare at him. His dark blue eyes danced with laughter. The blue t-shirt he wore made them seem even bluer. The sleeves fought for their life against his huge biceps. Goddamn, he was sexy for fifty-one and Harlan didn't think he had ever thought that before. Money kept people young. Plus, it was obvious Tanner worked out. He had a sexy belly on him, but Harlan was into that. Fuck. Why did he have to smell good?

"What's everyone's plans for the rest of the night?"

Everyone except Harlan made noises about needing to get home.

Tanner shook his head. "I come all the way here from Canada and none of you can make it past ten? I'm the oldest one here." He looked Harlan's way. "What about you?"

Harlan shrugged, trying not to look too enthusiastic. "I'm game for whatever. I haven't gotten too old to party yet."

Rider snorted. "You could stand to party a little less."

Tanner draped his arm across Harlan's shoulders. "Don't worry. I'll keep him in line."

"That's not as comforting as you obviously think," Ben muttered, making Tanner laugh.

Everyone said their goodbyes and headed en masse toward the door. Tanner's arm never left Harlan's shoulders. Then they were alone. The act fell away.

Tanner's gaze moved his way. A smirk touched his lips. "Alone at last."

Challenge always fired to life inside him whenever Tanner was around. "Oh dear. Do I need to break out my rape whistle?"

Tanner snorted so hard, it had to hurt. He choked on a laugh. "Everyone else likes me, you know? You're the only exception."

Harlan had to point out the obvious. "That's a broad assumption of yourself. But I never said I don't like you. I might have said you're a little too sure of yourself."

"Damn, Pot. Come, take a walk with this old kettle."

Harlan couldn't stop smiling. It was genuinely too much fun being with Tanner. He never knew what would come next. Harlan hoped it was him.

Money bought a lot of things. Actually, it bought most of everything. Tanner hadn't encountered much in his life that couldn't be his with enough zeros. He liked that Harlan's entire family seemed immune to that, sans their mother, of course. They were ballsy. It was refreshing. It made Tanner want them in his corner and watching his back. He didn't fear they would fuck him the first chance they got. Harlan was a bit of an exception. Tanner really wanted Harlan to fuck him.

Tanner had known Rider for a long time. Since Matt was a former hockey player, they had crossed paths too. It wasn't until Tanner had thrown Rider a surprise birthday party that he had finally met Harlan, and goddamn. Everything about him was sexual. He bled sensuality. His eyes constantly flashed with the promise of naughty things. He smirked in a way that made it clear he would be a ride no one would forget. Tanner had never instantly wanted anyone more.

He savored the feeling of Harlan tucked against his side as he led him down to the Chuckers' sideline bench. The closer they got to the ice, the colder the air got. Tanner needed the chill to cool his over-heated skin. Otherwise, he would send Harlan running for the hills. They sat on the bench.

"It's oddly amazing up close."

Tanner smiled at the wonder in Harlan's voice. It sounded the way Tanner felt when he thought about this team.

Harlan turned his head. His light blue eyes stole the air from Tanner's lungs. His nearly jet-black hair and light eyes combined to make him stunning. "Why a hockey team? I imagine you could own anything you want. Why this?"

Tanner shrugged. "I'm Canadian. They strap ice skates to our feet the moment we take our first steps. Hockey is in my blood. When this team went up for sale, I knew it was probably the only chance I'd get to own a piece of something I love. What about you? Why not hockey? That's the path your brothers chose."

A sexy smile touched Harlan's lips, drawing Tanner's gaze to his mouth. A day's worth of growth covered his jaw. His full lips were calling Tanner's name. "I've never been anything like my brothers. Hockey is no exception. Rider couldn't get away fast enough, and hockey was his ticket out. Matt has always been Mom's baby because he was soft enough for her to manipulate. She saw how much Rider made from his hockey career. So she pushed for Matt to do the same, hoping to bleed him dry. Thankfully, Slater seems to have put a stop to that since they married. Meanwhile, I was the middle child, so I went unnoticed. But I wanted to be like my dad." Harlan's sad smile moved Tanner. It was obvious Harlan had loved his father, and it hadn't been that long since he passed.

Tanner wanted to make it better. "I'd say you've accomplished that."

Harlan's smile turned laughing. "Some would say I accomplished it too well."

A laugh burst from Tanner. "Yeah, I've heard the rumors." Harlan's dad had been a huge womanizer. Word was Harlan was the same.

"Don't believe half of what you've heard. I don't have any bastard children running around. No matter what my brothers say."

Tanner wished he could say he hadn't heard that one, but he had. "It's three at last count, right?"

A loud groan burst from Harlan. He looked away and shook his head before meeting Tanner's gaze again. "Okay, so. The first one might have had a legitimate claim. There was enough of a chance that I did a paternity test. That kid isn't mine. The other two women making that claim, I've never even met. When I ignored their bullshit, they went to my parents. I guess they hoped my family would pay them off to spare some embarrassment or whatever. Little did they know my mom would rather die than have anyone call her a grandmother. Plus, there's very likely some kids running around out there that could call themselves my siblings. That was a Pandora's box best ignored by everyone."

Tanner couldn't stop smiling. Harlan's outrage was adorable. "So no kids?"

"Definitely not."

"So all football. No kids. Do you know how to skate, or did you pass on the hockey lessons?"

Harlan snorted. "Are you kidding me? My dad put us in as many sports as he could shove into a daily schedule. None of us had any sort of life until we went to college."

Tanner tilted his head toward the ice. "Would you like to skate with me?"

"It's been a while."

Good. That gave Tanner a reason to touch him. "I'll keep you upright."

Harlan's tongue shot out, wetting his lips in a way that drew the eye. Everything about him was a temptation. "Okay."

At Harlan's agreement, Tanner was on his feet in an instant. He was happy for any excuse to possibly hold Harlan. "Come on. Let's hunt down some skates."

Together, they headed down the tunnel to the locker room. The equipment manager hadn't left for the night. He was more than happy to find them skates. In minutes, they were out on the ice.

"Watch out. It's still torn up out here from the game. They won't clean it for a few more hours."

Harlan eyed the ice. For once, he didn't look as confident. "I probably should've thought this through. If I get hurt, that's my career."

Tanner hadn't considered that either. Harlan had a multimillion-dollar leg. He couldn't let Harlan twist an ankle. Tanner closed the distance between them. Facing him, he held Harlan's waist while skating backward. Harlan grabbed his shoulders and held on.

The longer they skated, the more comfortable everything felt. Not that Tanner ever felt uncomfortable. Sometimes he got the impression he made Harlan uneasy. It didn't feel that way now.

"When you asked what we were doing later, I never thought this was what you'd want to do with your night."

Damn. Now Tanner really wanted to know what Harlan had pictured them doing. "Honestly, I knew your brothers wouldn't want to hang out, so the offer was for you. Unfortunately, I get the impression you wouldn't want me to single you out in front of them."

Harlan cocked his head to one side. His gaze moved over Tanner's face as if working on a puzzle. "Why do you think that?"

Tanner didn't play games. "You don't look or speak to me when they're around unless I speak to you first. I figured you didn't want them to know you've spent time alone with me."

"You're my brother's boss. I don't want Rider to worry."

They weren't skating any longer, but neither of them pulled away. In the middle of the arena, they stood toe to toe, holding each other. "I'm not that bad of a guy."

Harlan smirked. "I am, and he knows it."

"You can't get me pregnant."

A loud laugh burst from Harlan, making Tanner smile. "I could try."

Tanner snorted. "I'd let you, but I don't think I'd ever see you again afterward."

Harlan's smile never dimmed. "You probably wouldn't."

Tanner held on to his smile, but Harlan confirming his fears stung. He took Harlan's hand. "Then we should find something safer to do."

Harlan didn't pull away as Tanner led him off the ice. The guy kept him confused. He would cut his losses for the night. It didn't look as if Harlan would ever be his.

CHAPTER TWO

SATIN SHEETS ENVELOPED HIM. Soft light filled the room. Harlan buried his head beneath the pillow. He didn't want to get up and face the day. It wasn't often he got to be lazy. Tanner's second home in New Orleans was a third of the size of his home in Canada. So it was still massive. After a night of drinking, they had decided it would be best if Harlan spent the night with him—in one of the spare bedrooms—rather than showing up at Rider's place in the middle of the night three sheets to the wind. While Harlan always believed he lived in luxury, his life had no comparison to Tanner's. Everything was the absolute best, especially the service.

The scent of bacon and coffee filled the room. Someone had quietly left breakfast for him while he slept. Now his stomach warred with his mind. He still wanted to sleep, but the food smelled amazing. Harlan had expected to be sick as hell this morning. It seemed that top-of-the-line alcohol went down and stayed down smoother.

A soft knock landed on the door.

"Come in."

Harlan sat up as the door opened. The satin sheets pooled in his lap. His nipples hardened in the cool room. Tanner stepped inside the room, looking extra yummy for someone who had been drinking all night. His hair was perfectly styled. Once again, a t-shirt strained across his chest and arms.

He smiled. "Hey. Did I wake you?"

Harlan ran his fingers through his hair, wishing he looked half as hot first thing in the morning. "Nah. I was just being lazy. It looks like you've been up a while."

"I don't really sleep. What are your plans for today?"

"Technically, I'm on vacation, so I don't have any."

Tanner kept his gaze locked on Harlan's face. Harlan might not have noticed how carefully Tanner didn't eye his body if he didn't want him to so badly. "After you eat and whatever, would you like to go gambling?"

A smile exploded across Harlan's face. Gambling wasn't something he did often. He didn't like going alone and no one else he knew was willing to blow money for likely no return. "I'd love to." Harlan realized something important. His smile slipped. "My luggage is at Rider's place."

"It's right there." Tanner pointed toward a spot near the window. Harlan turned his head. Sure enough, his luggage waited for him. "I sent someone to pick it up this morning."

Harlan shook his head. "Awful damn sure of yourself, aren't you?" He turned his head in time to catch Tanner's gaze moving down his body.

Tanner met his stare again, unfazed by getting caught enjoying the view. "It's luggage. You needed clothes, and I knew you could take your bags straight back to Rider's, if you want." A slow smirk touched his lips. "But I'm hoping you won't."

"I'll eat breakfast and then we'll see."

With a smile, Tanner shook his head. "I'll leave you to it."

Harlan climbed from the bed. "You don't have to do that. It's nice to have company when you eat."

This time, with Harlan on his feet and wearing nothing but his underwear, Tanner didn't hide the way his gaze raked down Harlan's body. "If that's what you want."

The husky note to Tanner's voice nearly had Harlan embarrassing them both. He wanted Tanner, and it was so fucking wrong. As Harlan had already pointed out, Tanner was Rider's boss. Tanner might claim that didn't matter, but Harlan knew better. When feelings got hurt, all bets were off. There was also an age gap and a huge distance between them. Harlan lived in California. Tanner's home was in Toronto. That was a hell of a trip. Plus, Harlan was considering all those details, which meant he wanted more than one night. He genuinely liked Tanner, and Harlan had met dozens of men like him. Tanner always got what he wanted. The moment he had Harlan, they would never speak again. Harlan knew it was true, because he was that guy too. He didn't do relationships.

"Your mood shifted so hard, it sucked the oxygen from the room."

Tanner was too damn observant. Harlan forced a smile to his face as he took a seat at the tiny table where his food waited. "I'm not a morning person."

Tanner didn't budge from his spot near the door. "I don't think that's it. Maybe I should leave you alone after all."

Fuck. Harlan wasn't trying to ruin their friendship, which was exactly the problem. He really wanted to wreck their friendship, but in a different way.

"You're not twelve, Tanner. Sit the fuck down."

At his order, Tanner moved to the chair across from Harlan. "Damn. Okay, bossy."

Harlan bit back a smile as he eyed the tray. The plate was covered, and the coffee waited to be poured. While he lifted the lid, Tanner filled Harlan's cup. It was a comfortable moment—like they always shared breakfast.

Harlan snagged the bacon. "Do you want these eggs? I'd hate for them to go to waste, but I'm allergic."

Tanner accepted the plate. "I'll make sure my staff knows so they can accommodate you next time." He motioned toward the bacon Harlan held. "Are you okay to eat that since it touched the eggs? I can have them bring you something fresh."

It was nice as hell having someone worry about him. "It's fine. I can tolerate a minuscule amount."

With a nod, Tanner doctored Harlan's coffee for him. Harlan ate his bacon and watched. Something grew inside his chest. They'd had coffee together before. The fact that Tanner had obviously paid attention to how he liked his drink and remembered... wow. That was the kind of thing that had him in trouble. Tanner was selfish and spoiled, yet he showed more care for him than the people who claimed to love him over the years.

Harlan wanted to show him the same care. "Tell me about yourself. I know you told me you're an only child, but you've never talked about your parents or anything like that." Harlan supposed he could have Googled Tanner, but he wanted to hear about him from Tanner's mouth. Google wouldn't show him Tanner's heart.

A sweet smile touched Tanner's lips. "Hmm. Well, my parents were a collision of two tycoons. My father made billions in the software industry. My mom made billions in the cosmetics industry. They decidedly did not love each other. It was more like they didn't fear each other taking the other for a ride. Plus, what's better than having several billions? Having twice that." Tanner took a bite of eggs and swallowed before continuing. "I never saw my father. He had produced an heir who didn't embarrass him. That's all he needed from me. My mom was a different story. She had come from nothing to earn everything she had. Her mom had been a single mother in a day when it was damn near impossible to raise a child alone as a woman. My mom wanted me from day one and made sure I always knew it." He winked. "You can blame her for how spoiled I am. Dad passed about fifteen years ago. Mom passed five years ago. I stay busy keeping their companies thriving, but things have been very quiet with her gone."

Harlan was fascinated by Tanner. This side of him was scary amazing. "So you run both companies?"

Tanner nodded. "Obviously, I have people in place to handle day-to-day operations, but I still have full ownership of both companies."

"Wow. Plus two hockey teams between pro and sled. That sounds exhausting."

Tanner took another bite of eggs and shrugged. "Not really, but sometimes, yeah. Like I said, with people like Rider in my life, it makes everything easier." A wry smile touched his lips. "When I can force myself not to ride all their asses, that is. I fully admit I'm a huge pain to work for, but I pay well."

Harlan wouldn't admit he had heard the nightmare stories from Rider about working for Tanner. Rider still considered Tanner like family, despite his obnoxious ways. To Harlan, that said a lot about Tanner.

"What about you?" Tanner asked, turning the conversation Harlan's way. "You'll be thirty-four next week. How many more years do you plan to give to football?"

"How did you know my birthday is next week?"

Tanner's brow furrowed. "You told me last year at Rider's birthday party."

He was in so much trouble with this one. "I'd forgotten that conversation." A thought hit. "Damn. I missed your birthday. I could've made the trip to Canada. The season had already ended."

Tanner shrugged. "When you get to be my age, there's no one left to remember." He finished Harlan's eggs like he hadn't just made a heartbreaking confession.

"If it makes you feel any better, with Dad gone, I doubt anyone will think of me either. Except you, of course," he added. "Obviously, you remembered." A thought hit. "It's only been a month. We should celebrate. I'm a little late, but better late than never for a birthday bash."

The way Tanner eyed him in silence had feelings stirring. "You don't have to do that. I don't need anything."

Harlan stood. "Birthdays aren't about needs. They're about celebrating you. Fifty-one. Hmm. What should we do?"

"You could spank me."

A laugh burst from Harlan. "Let me grab a shower and we'll figure something out."

"So, just to be clear, spanking is not off the table, right?"

Harlan couldn't stop smiling. Tanner was so much fun. "Maybe if you're good."

"Damn. I'm never good."

Harlan shook his head and headed for the bathroom. Soft laughter filled the room behind him. Harlan's face hurt from smiling. This would be a good day. Every day spent with Tanner always was.

It was the worst of hells. Harlan looked sexy as fuck. He had started the day parading around in his underwear. From there, he had spent the day touching Tanner as much as possible. Goddamn. It might not have been purposeful. Tanner couldn't tell, but he sure as fuck noticed every time Harlan's hands landed on his body. That was why Tanner was on his third drink in the seventh circle of hell. He had lost a lot of money and then won it back. They had played craps and poker. Slots had oddly been more in his favor than either of those games. Harlan had been right at his side, tossing back drinks twice as quickly as Tanner. He knew he needed to slow down before he lost his head. Everything already had a bit of a surreal edge to it. Not to mention, his tongue went loose when he drank too much. He very much feared telling Harlan exactly how he felt. Tanner was obsessed. He had to sober up fast.

"Oh, look. Do you hear that music?"

A laugh burst from Tanner. "I'm pretty sure that's two different senses, but yeah. There's a nightclub attached to the casino."

Harlan slapped his arm. "Holy shit. We should go dancing. I haven't been dancing in years."

Tanner rubbed his arm, feigning pain. "You're a hitter when you're drunk."

Harlan snorted. "This isn't drunk... yet."

With a laugh, Tanner linked arms with Harlan and headed toward the club. "If sexy wants to dance, then sexy gets what he wants."

"You're funny."

Tanner looked his way. "Why? Do you not think you're sexy?"

Harlan made a wild motion with his arm. "Oh. I know I'm sexy. It was just an observation. You're funny."

Damn it. He didn't want to be funny. Tanner wanted to be sexy too. Getting old sucked. No one looked at him as closely any longer. Now he was just funny. Damn. A cover charge later, darkness engulfed them. Music thumped. Bodies gyrated. Harlan hadn't been joking. He immediately dragged Tanner onto the dance floor. It had been a long time. Any trepidation he had fell away once they were grinding against each other. The music was the perfect mixture of fast and slow. Sensual. Tanner was mesmerized.

Harlan held his stare as their bodies moved against each other. Tanner suddenly felt completely sober. His hand wandered. It was out of his control. The cut lines of Harlan's body were too much of a temptation. He went from exploring the hard planes of Harlan's back to sliding south until he held the tightest and most perfect ass. Harlan didn't pull away or say no. In fact, they seemed to get even closer. Then the music slowed a little more. A love song filled the air. Harlan's arms were around his neck. His every breath brushed Tanner's ear.

Tanner was so aroused, he couldn't think. He released Harlan's ass only because he wanted to hold Harlan as closely as possible. His hands still didn't stop moving. He kept massaging Harlan's back and sides, needing to memorize the way he felt as he moved against him.

"I like you a lot more than I should."

Even with the loud music playing, the soft words against his ear couldn't be missed. Tanner's eyelids slid closed. He savored the moment. "Same."

"You know we could never work."

Fuck that. Tanner could absolutely make them work. His money bought freedom. He could do whatever. Be wherever. He would for Harlan. Tanner just needed a chance to prove it. He needed Harlan to let go and cross the line with him.

Tanner kissed the spot beneath Harlan's ear. "I'm willing to try. You're worth it to me."

A sexy chuckle caressed the shell of his ear. "The moment you've had a night with me, I'll never see you again. I know the score."

That statement should have enraged Tanner. Instead, it just made him sad. For both of them. He took Harlan's hand and walked away from the dance floor. Harlan needed more alcohol. Tanner needed anything at all to wash the bitterness from his mouth.

CHAPTER THREE

HIS SHIRT WAS TWISTED beneath him, driving him nuts. Harlan yanked, trying to untangle himself without fully waking. He wasn't ready to face the day. Something warm stirred beside him. Harlan lifted his head and peeked open one eye. On top of the covers, on his stomach, Tanner slept peacefully. Harlan eyed the room. He was about ninety percent certain they were in Tanner's bed. They were fully dressed, so there was comfort in that.

His shoulders relaxed. He rolled over and cuddled the pillow. There was zero reason he couldn't go back to sleep. They had obviously made it home safely. On the edge of dozing off, a buzzing penetrated his peace. With his eyes still closed, Harlan patted the bedside table until he found his phone. He fully intended to take one quick peek to make sure it wasn't an emergency and then turn off his phone. That expensive liquor hadn't gone down quite as smoothly this time. Harlan needed another four hours to recover, at least. He lifted one eyelid again and checked the face. He had missed a hundred and forty-seven calls and eighty texts. That had Harlan's attention.

"What the fuck?" The phone didn't immediately recognize his face to unlock the device, proving how rough he looked. There were too many different numbers in the call log for Harlan to guess at the urgency. Harlan focused on the texts instead. He read Rider's first. If anyone would get straight to the point and know the lowdown, it would be him.

> Rider: *How in the fuck could you marry my boss?*

Harlan sat up straight like he had been poked with a cattle prod. He kept reading.

> Rider: *Tanner? Tanner Paige of all people? He's nearly twenty years older than you. He's an even bigger narcissist than Mom.*

Okay. That irritated Harlan no matter his level of shock. Tanner was nothing like their mom. He scrubbed his hand over his face. There had to be a mistake. This had to be a prank. Something rough scraped his skin as he fought to wipe the exhaustion from his face. He looked at his hand. There was a gorgeous wedding ring on the ring finger of his left hand. His heart raced. Each breath came harder than the last. He searched his memory, going over every detail of the night. They had gone to the casino and then to a club. Things had gotten a little too hot while dancing, so they had moved to the bar. There had been drinks. Laughter. So many fucking drinks. He couldn't breathe. Harlan needed a paper bag stat.

"Oh my god. Holy hell. What did we do?"

He punched Tanner in the arm. "What in the hell did we do?"

Tanner's head lifted. His hair stood in every direction. Stupidly, he looked even sexier when sleep-mussed. No. Harlan couldn't think like that. He needed Tanner to tell him it was a joke.

"I'm awake. What's up?" He didn't sound the least bit awake, but Harlan couldn't worry about that now.

"What did we do?" Even Harlan heard the panic in his voice.

Tanner's head turned from side to side. "We're both dressed, so I'm guessing nothing."

"Why did I miss a million texts about us getting married? And I'm wearing a wedding band." He looked at Tanner's hand. "Oh my God. You are too."

Tanner looked at his hand. "Huh. I thought that was a dream."

"What?" The screech took even Harlan by surprise. He had never been this panicked.

"Okay. I'm sitting up. We'll figure this out." He rolled. His shirt moved upward as he went, showing off the delicious skin beneath. Harlan had to stop. He could not lust after this man. Harlan definitely couldn't be married to him.

Tanner pushed to his feet. He stretched, as if he didn't have a care in the world. Tanner grabbed his phone. A stack of papers sat beneath. Tanner paused and cocked his head to the side. He set his phone on the bed and picked up the papers. Tanner spent a moment eyeing each page. Finally, Tanner turned a page Harlan's way. "At least we look happy." It was a photo of them at the altar, kissing.

He turned another paper Harlan's way. "Yep. Married." It was a wedding certificate. There was no missing the official gold seal and both their signatures.

The wind left Harlan. The confirmation brought an odd calm over him. Tanner didn't seem panicked at all. Surely, that meant he didn't need to freak out either. Tanner was in charge of massive corporations. He would know what to do. Tanner would handle everything. Except Tanner kept silently flipping through what appeared to be the pictures of their wedding. His silence was a bit frightening.

"Say something."

Tanner glanced up. "Sorry. Are you okay?"

Was he? Harlan assessed his emotions. What had him the most freaked out? This was obviously something they could undo... except it seemed the whole world knew already. He didn't want to embarrass Tanner. His shoulders fell.

Tanner set the papers aside and climbed onto the bed. He snagged Harlan's waist and settled down, cuddling him against his chest.

"It's okay. Say what's in your head."

"I don't remember anything." It surprised Harlan for that to be the first admission to pop from his mouth.

Tanner stroked his back, comforting him. "How can I fix it?"

Harlan took several breaths. His muscles relaxed. Without thinking, he shoved his arm beneath Tanner's shirt, looking for warmth. Tanner grabbed a handful of covers and tugged them over them.

"You're so calm." Honestly, it was catching.

Tanner hummed. The sound vibrated against Harlan's ear. "If I'm going to do something completely crazy, at least it happened with a friend I trust."

Harlan closed his eyes. That was true. Things could be so much worse. It occurred to him his panic might have been somewhat insulting. Now that he could think a little clearer, Harlan had to admit it was flattering the way Tanner seemed unbothered.

"Sorry I freaked out."

Tanner traced the shell of Harlan's ear. He was putting Harlan to sleep with his soothing touch. "It's okay. I know it's scary not to remember what you've done."

It was like Tanner reached into his head and pulled out the heart of the matter. He might have done anything while too inebriated to know better.

"We'll be okay."

Harlan nodded at Tanner's reassurance. Sleep weighed heavily on him. His breathing deepened. With Tanner's fingertips trailing up and down his jaw, Harlan let the darkness swallow him.

Tanner listened to the shower run. He kept his mind blank. There was an odd peace inside him he hadn't expected. If he had woken up married to anyone else, he would have a team of lawyers in his living room, squashing any chance of this standing. He would protect his assets with every fiber of his being and have an annulment by sundown. Instead, he was simply... fine. There was no panic or fear. Instead, the idea of Harlan as his husband grew on him a little more by the second. They obviously had a lot to figure out, but Tanner didn't want to face it right away. He needed to marinate over it.

Harlan stepped from the bathroom, wearing nothing but a towel. Tanner didn't hide his interest. Harlan was sexy as fuck, and he had married Tanner.

Tanner didn't hesitate to use the situation to his advantage. "I've been thinking. We were kissing in all those photos. Maybe we should try it. It might jog some memories."

Harlan flashed him a wry look. "Uh, huh."

Tanner tried looking innocent. "Really? Apparently, it's already happened several times. What's one more? I'm your husband, remember?"

Harlan laughed. He crossed the room to where Tanner still sat in his towel on the bed where he had been since he showered. "How much longer do you think we can keep our phones off before my brothers bang down the door?"

Tanner shrugged. "They'll end up cooling their heels until I tell the staff we're ready to accept visitors. No one gets past my security."

Harlan stood over Tanner. His hands landed on Tanner's bare shoulders. The air changed in the room. Tanner's hands moved of their own accord. He ran his palms up the back of Harlan's thighs. His gaze never wavered from Harlan's face. Harlan dipped his head and touched his lips to Tanner's. For a moment, time stood still. They shared each other's air. Tanner broke first. He nibbled Harlan's bottom lip, testing its firmness. The bed dipped next to his hip as Harlan set one knee on the bed. His mouth opened. Their tongues met. Heat exploded between them. Harlan straddled his lap. While holding Harlan, Tanner stood and took Harlan down on the bed. Their towels didn't stand a chance in the bustle. Tanner held Harlan's wrists above his head as he explored his mouth. Harlan didn't fight him for control. Tanner knew he could be too much. That knowledge did him no good now that he had Harlan beneath him. His intensity kicked up to a scary level. Their kiss was almost violent. They came at each other like they were starved. Tanner didn't know where this was headed. It was supposed to be just a kiss. Maybe Harlan would stop him any second. If he didn't, Tanner wouldn't. He had wanted this for too long.

"Where's the lube? I need to be inside you."

Tanner didn't need to hear anything else. He dove for the bedside table. Their desperation was unlike anything he had experienced before. Harlan's mouth never left some part of Tanner's skin, even as Harlan rolled on a condom. When Tanner sat on Harlan's dick, Harlan made a sound that nearly pulled an orgasm from him. If anyone had ever wanted him like this, Tanner couldn't recall it. This entire situation was new for him, and Tanner hadn't thought there was anything new left in the world for him. With his money, nothing had ever been out of his reach. But Harlan didn't give a shit about his money. He wasn't impressed by Tanner. Desire was the only reason he let Tanner ride his dick, and it was the most addicting experience of Tanner's life. The feeling in his chest was bigger than anything he knew before now. He couldn't let Harlan go.

Harlan kissed and bit. He used Tanner. His fingers dug into Tanner's ass cheeks as he lifted and pulled while pumping upward. He took Tanner's asshole, and Tanner loved every second. Their thrusts were almost violent. They were a storm, crashing against each other. Harlan sucked Tanner's neck hard as he fucked him even harder. All Tanner could do was whine and take it. With his eyes squeezed closed, he focused on every sensation. Harlan pounded at the perfect angle. The sound of skin slapping skin mixed with the building pressure. Tanner's mind was a mess. He needed this. His muscles tensed. Tanner held his breath. A cry tore from his lips when the orgasm hit. It was so powerful, he couldn't control the sounds he made. His entire body jerked as he shot cum on

Harlan's stomach. Harlan didn't let up the pace. Hard and fast, he rammed his cock inside Tanner, taking what he wanted. Tanner's body twitched. He saw heaven. Then Harlan cried out against his throat. The sound nearly sent Tanner over the edge again.

Their movements slowed as they rocked out the final waves. Wheezing breaths filled the air, proving how hard they had worked to blow as fast as possible. Tanner's pulse sounded loud in his ears as he tried catching his breath. He knew he squished Harlan beneath him, but he couldn't move. Harlan wasn't making any moves to remedy the situation either.

"Holy shit. That was…"

Tanner nodded at Harlan's assessment. He fully agreed. There were no words.

"I swear I'll move in a second."

He felt Harlan's laughter. "No hurry. You can stay there forever if you'd like. Hell, you can do whatever you want. That was... wow."

Tanner chuckled as he mustered the energy to roll away, freeing Harlan. They both stared at the ceiling while catching their breath. At the same time, they burst out laughing. They turned their heads and their gazes collided. Harlan's eyes swam with happiness. Tanner didn't doubt he looked the same. They were both pretty crazy. Together, they were totally insane. Tanner couldn't imagine being with anyone else ever again.

This was his husband. The idea grew on Tanner by the second. He fully recognized exactly how many strings his money had pulled for them to get married on a whim last night. That alone proved Tanner had wanted this pretty damn badly. As independent as Harlan was, he had to have wanted it too to have agreed, inebriated or not. Deep down, this was what they craved. In the morning light, it was still what Tanner wanted. That meant there was only one course of action. Tanner had to get all the way in the way of untangling this until Harlan had the same realizations. In his heart, Tanner felt maybe they were meant to be. Soon, Harlan would see it too.

CHAPTER FOUR

IF HE DIDN'T HAVE Tanner at his side, Harlan might have been nervous. Security had alerted them of Rider's arrival. They had taken their time cleaning up and dressing. Things had moved even slower because they kept stopping to kiss. It was like Harlan moved through a dream. He knew any second he would wake up and everything would feel incredibly insane. But like any dream, nothing felt wrong because it wasn't real. In no time, this would be over. They would look back on this and laugh. For now, Harlan clung to the wisps of the natural high. Being with Tanner was exhilarating, which was exactly how Harlan knew it couldn't last. Someone like Tanner didn't get tied down like this. Harlan was the same. They were unique to each other for now. Soon enough, that would fade.

Together, they headed for the sitting room, prepared to face the firing squad together. As they approached the doorway, Tanner's hand landed on the small of his back. It was the tiniest gesture, but he knew they looked like a team as they stepped into the room. Rider looked thunderous. Ben sat on the loveseat, looking completely unfazed. Of course, he was the calmer of the two.

"What in the fuck are you two doing?"

At Rider's question, they exchanged a glance. A silent message passed between them. Harlan would handle his brother.

"It seems you already know the answer to that, or you wouldn't be here." He moved to the couch and sat. Tanner filled the spot next to him. He draped his arm across the back, crowding Harlan's space and showing a united front.

Rider pinched the spot between his eyes. "This is so fucking wrong." He dropped his hand and focused on Harlan. "Exactly how long has this been going on?"

Harlan didn't know how to answer that one.

Thankfully, Tanner obviously did. "Since I threw that surprise party for you."

Rider dropped into the spot next to Ben on the loveseat. He looked between them. "That's almost a year. Neither of you said anything."

Harlan shrugged. "It's not like we talk. Why would I tell you this?" As the words left his lips, he realized he was kind of pissed. Rider never called and asked how he was. Now he was here, demanding answers. "I also don't recall hearing anything about you getting married until Mom told me."

Rider didn't take the bait. "There's no way this is for real. What are you two up to with this? Tanner is too spoiled to ever settle down and you're too much like Dad."

Oooh, Harlan was good and pissed off now. "What's that supposed to mean?"

Rider's light blue eyes softened. "You know what I mean, Harlan. He never stayed faithful to Mom. With the number of women who claim I have nieces and nephews running around, you can't tell me this marriage will be any different from theirs. You can't even take care of those kids and they're your blood. Tanner will be acting like Mom in under six months. I care about both of you, and I can already see you two hating each other's guts in under a year. This won't end well."

With every word Rider spoke, Harlan's anger grew. While he recognized he had never truly defended himself against any baby-making claims, he hadn't thought he needed to with his family. "It seems you made up your mind about me a long time ago, so this seems like a pointless visit. Go home and go back to forgetting you have brothers. You're better at that than this meddling."

"Harlan, I know I've—"

Harlan swiped his hand through the air. "No. I don't want to hear it. You ran away from this family as fast as you could and didn't look back. Now you've decided to show up just in time to prove you don't know me at all. If you did, you'd never accuse me of abandoning a kid. I don't want to defend myself anymore about those false claims. You don't deserve to hear me say I've been struggling against people who tell lies just because they want money. All the while, I've had nowhere to turn. Until this moment, I didn't fully understand why I've felt that way. Thank you for clearing up the matter. I have nowhere because I have no one." Harlan knew he had to look as outraged as he felt and sounded. He couldn't stop.

"Tanner is the only person to ever listen to me and believe me without question. All the while, my so-called family has walked around like I'm their secret shame. As far as I'm concerned, you don't deserve to know about my relationship with Tanner any more than any other detail of my life. Go home and believe whatever the fuck you want. You're not needed here."

Ben looked genuinely sad.

Rider's expression had closed halfway through Harlan's speech and hadn't changed. He stood. "I'm sorry." For a moment, his mask slipped, and Harlan saw his brother. Sadness washed over him. For both of them. They were who their parents had made them, which was two very different people. Without making excuses on top of his apology, Rider focused on Tanner. "Thank you for being there for my brother. I hope you two have an amazing life together." He turned away and held his hand out for Ben.

Ben accepted. He cast them a quick glance before letting Rider pull him to his feet. "Congratulations." Without another word, the pair left them behind.

Harlan stared straight ahead, focusing on nothing. Seeing nothing. He regretted every word he had said. Unfortunately, that didn't make them any less true. Tanner was the only person who treated him like he was proud to know him. He was heartsick, and the worst part was, this marriage wasn't real. Tanner would make it go away, and Rider would think he had been right all along. For the first time since he woke to this new reality, Harlan questioned himself. A drunk mind reached for sober dreams. Maybe he really wanted this marriage after all.

Tanner sat in silence with his arm over Harlan's shoulders. He brushed his thumb back and forth across a cut valley there that kept him fascinated. He didn't know what to expect. It was very possible Harlan would explode at any second. It was equally possible he would shake it off and act like he hadn't just poured out his heart. Either way, Tanner was here for it. He would follow Harlan's lead.

"As much as it pains me to admit, I like you a lot more than anyone else."

A laugh burst from Tanner at Harlan's words. He could be such an asshole. Tanner loved his company. "The feeling is mutual."

Harlan didn't laugh, nor did he look Tanner's way. "I said that to say this. I can't let Rider be right about us."

Everything inside Tanner froze. He didn't dare hope. He had thought he would have to use his lawyer and the courts as a stalling method. "What do you mean?"

Harlan finally turned his head and met Tanner's stare. There was so much pain in Harlan's eyes, it hurt Tanner's chest. "What can I do to convince you to stay married? I don't mean permanently, and I don't expect you to change your life or anything. I just don't want Rider to have another excuse to think less of me." He looked away. "That probably sounds dumb as hell. I need to let you go. None of this is your problem."

Tanner kissed the shell of Harlan's ear. He didn't want this moment to be about Rider, but he would use him as an excuse. His lips moved to the spot behind Harlan's ear. He pressed a light kiss there. "You're incredibly beautiful and amazing. Anyone would be honored to be your husband, especially me. I won't embarrass you."

Harlan drew a shaky-sounding breath.

Tanner knew he had him. He touched Harlan's chin, hoping for his attention. Harlan didn't hesitate. He turned his head and let Tanner have the kiss he wanted. Their tongues stroked. Desire crackled in the air. Triumph roared through Tanner. He wasn't a fool. He knew they had a huge mess of complications in front of them. Not only did they live in two different countries, but their homes were also over twenty-five hundred miles apart. He could relocate and live here, but New Orleans honestly wasn't much closer to Los Angeles. Harlan had a career people would die to have. He couldn't give that up for Tanner, and Tanner would never ask that of him. He had a few months until his season started. Tanner would fix everything somehow. They would figure out something. What Tanner wouldn't do was let Harlan get away. He needed to give Rider a raise. In a span of minutes, Rider had sealed a deal Tanner had been working toward for a year. He had practically handed Harlan to him, gift wrapped. Now Tanner had to find a way to make it last forever.

CHAPTER FIVE

Harlan had never truly considered what life with Tanner—day in and day out—would look like. He thought he understood what it was like to have money. Harlan had not been prepared for what leveling up would do to his life. If and when this marriage ended, he would be broke from the lawyer's fees in under a year. It felt like everyone he had ever crossed paths with came out of the woodwork, staking claims. His mom had gone from a semi-annual pain in his ass to an absolute terror overnight. Whereas he had thought Matt marrying a duke had been bad, it was nothing by comparison. The idea that her children would leave her in poverty, which was the most ridiculous claim in the history of claims, sent her over the edge. Matters weren't helped by the fact that she had hoped to be the one who landed Tanner. His head pounded just thinking about it.

Life with Tanner, excluding those things, was so much more amazing than he ever dreamed. Tanner was all the things Harlan expected. Spoiled, controlling, and demanding. Harlan just did as he pleased, and Tanner always broke first. The arrangement benefited them both. Tanner needed someone in his life telling him no. Unfortunately, Harlan's nos were getting less and less.

"Aren't you glad you said yes to this?"

With Tanner saying the words against his neck, Harlan had a hard time saying no. From a private box in Vegas, they watched the Chuckers play the Golden Sabres. With his chest pressed against Harlan's back and his arms wrapped around Harlan's waist, they stood for the whole world to see. Phones had pointed their way several times. A few times, he had seen TV cameras swing their way. Tanner never stopped holding him. To all the world, they looked like the happiest of newlyweds. Two people deeply in love. One of those things was true, at least. Harlan had to admit, Tanner played the perfect husband. It wouldn't last. Harlan didn't expect that either. Neither of them had expected this or meant for it to happen. They couldn't exactly expect loyalty.

"Do you travel for games often?"

He felt Tanner shrug at the question. "Aside from New Orleans, no. We're here for a reason." He kissed Harlan's ear. "Do you see number twenty-two? He's only nineteen."

"Bernier?"

Tanner nodded. "Storm Bernier. He's from Canada too. So we have that."

Harlan studied Twenty-two's moves. He was fast on the ice and his shots were like lightning. "There're a few accuracy issues, but in another year, he'll be coming for Medvedkov's records."

"Exactly. I want him before he hits that point and moves out of my price range."

"You have a price range?" Even Harlan heard the laughter in his voice.

Tanner chuckled. "Hmm. Well, let me rephrase that. Moves from what I'm willing to pay. I have to be reasonable."

Harlan nodded. "How do you intend to steal him?"

Tanner's hand moved from Harlan's stomach to his chest. Harlan fought the urge to close his eyes and savor the moment. Tanner held him more than he had ever been held in his life. He hadn't realized how starved for actual affection he had been until Tanner gave it to him—like it was second nature. "His contract is up at the end of this season. I've invited him to join us for a private meeting in the hotel's casino later tonight. I reserved a high-roller room. It's very unlikely anyone will know we talked. I'd like to keep it that way. If Vegas realizes I'm interested, they might bid to keep him at a higher price just to drive up the cost of the contract."

He found Tanner fascinating. Most people thought he was hands off with his teams since Rider ran everything, but no. Tanner loved the sport. He knew everything about it and picked up on details about players others might miss. His observant nature came with other perks as well. Harlan's sex life had never been so good.

"You said he's meeting us. Are you sure you want me to go? I know this is business."

"Yeah. Our business."

Tanner was forever saying things like that, and Harlan didn't know how to feel. The way they had gotten married, cut out any prenups, mixing their lives in a way that didn't always sit right with Harlan. This marriage was temporary. Harlan would never try to go after any of Tanner's assets. But Tanner talked as if everything was theirs now and Harlan didn't know how to act. So he didn't. "Okay."

Tanner kissed his ear again, as if praising him for agreeing.

The buzzer sounded. Vegas beat them by one with the winning shot going to Storm Bernier. It seemed Tanner knew what he was doing. Harlan was just along for the ride.

Tanner hadn't planned to set up a meeting with Storm until after the end of the season. This gave him a chance to jet Harlan to Vegas. They were close enough to LA; they would head to Harlan's place for a few weeks too. Tanner hoped that would lead to them making some long-term decisions. He didn't want to live apart when football started again for the year.

Tanner also hadn't thought of doing business in a casino. Then Harlan had married him in one. Now they were good luck to him.

"I didn't think about you being under twenty-one when I suggested we meet here."

Storm's green eyes flashed with laughter. "It's all good. I don't plan to stay long. No offense. My team is partying at a different hotel nearby."

"I promise I won't take up too much of your time."

Harlan leaned closer and touched his lips to Tanner's ear. "I'm going to find a restroom. I'll be back in a minute."

Tanner stole a quick kiss before Harlan got away. "Hurry back." He focused on Storm. Storm's gaze followed Harlan, giving Tanner permission to return to watching his husband. Harlan immediately got stopped right outside the doorway. The high-roller room turned out to be across from the sports betting room. Several people asked for selfies. Harlan stopped and obliged them all. Tanner smiled at the sight. Sometimes he forgot his husband was famous. When he looked back Storm's way. He found Storm studying him.

"It's nice to see someone in your position openly loving their husband. Representation matters." He changed the subject before Tanner caught his breath from Storm dropping the L word. "I take it this meeting is about my contract ending with Vegas."

Tanner nodded, scrambling to recover from being accused of loving Harlan. "Yes. I'd love for you to come check out New Orleans. I think you'd fit right in with my team, and you could learn a lot from Medvedkov. You'd be on a cup-winning team. Vegas can't level up your career the way I can."

Storm nodded. "Except this has been my team for two years and they've already offered a new contract."

A chuckle slipped from Tanner. "New Orleans and Vegas may as well be the same town. They're both unbearably hot party towns crawling with homeless people."

They shared a smile. "Nothing like home, eh?"

Tanner laughed as Storm's Canadian accent thickened. "No. Definitely not."

Storm's gaze slid toward the doorway again.

Tanner turned his head. Harlan was back and trapped again, taking more pictures.

"How do you two make it work, living so far apart? California is a long way from Toronto."

It was obvious Storm had looked into him before this meeting. He wished the question didn't glitch his brain. Tanner couldn't admit he had no idea. As far as the world knew, they had been a couple longer than the two months they'd been married.

Thankfully, Storm seemed to answer his own question before Tanner could come up with a lie. "I suppose you have the freedom to travel with him anywhere he goes." Storm sounded almost sad. He met Tanner's stare again. "I'll come check out the city this summer during the off season. My agent and I have already decided not to settle on a contract until I have time to weigh my options between seasons."

"That's fair. I have your number. We can set up something in a couple of months."

"Sounds good." Storm stood and shook Tanner's hand. "It was nice meeting you."

"You as well."

With a final nod, Storm headed for the door. He paused outside where Harlan stood. They exchanged a few words and then Storm took over, captivating the crowd so Harlan could get away.

Harlan headed Tanner's way, wearing a huge grin. He was so beautiful. Tanner couldn't tear his eyes away. He had won the husband lottery. Proud wasn't a strong enough word to describe how he felt.

"Lost him already, huh?"

Tanner realized he smiled every bit as brightly as Harlan. "Oh, to be young. There's a party going on somewhere with his name on it."

Harlan reclaimed his seat, pulling it closer as he sat. "How did it go?"

"He's agreed to check out the town this summer."

Harlan nodded. "Is that good sign?"

Tanner shrugged. "It's hard to say. All I can do now is wait."

A wicked-looking smirk touched Harlan's lips. He snagged the front of Tanner's t-shirt, towing him closer. "Whatever shall you do in the meantime?"

"I can think of one person."

Harlan chuckled as he brushed his lips across Tanner's. A thought hit Tanner. "You know you're the only person, right? We haven't really set boundaries for this marriage."

Harlan turned serious, showing the conversation the gravity it deserved. He eyed Tanner, making him a little nervous. Tanner knew Harlan might not want to be tied down exclusively.

When Harlan didn't answer right away, Tanner's tongue got the best of him. "I suppose you don't want something like that. You're not old like me and you're on the road a lot."

"I want that."

Harlan's quietly spoken words brought Tanner's ramblings to a halt. His pulse pounded in his ears. He was scared to hope. Every day this marriage got a little realer. "Are you sure?" He hated to keep giving Harlan outs, but he needed to know Harlan chose this because he chose Tanner.

"I'm sure." He pulled a face. "Honestly, I've been thinking about this one a lot lately. In a few months, I'll be headed to summer training. What happens then? Do we go our separate ways and act like we're not married?"

"I don't want that." The confession shot from Tanner, sounding desperate.

Harlan smiled. "I don't either. Obviously, we didn't plan for life to go in this direction, but I don't want to be my dad." He paused. His expression turned intense. "And I don't want to be married to someone like him. I give my mom a lot of shit, but he's the reason she is the way she is. She put up with a lot of shit before eventually deciding if she couldn't have his faithfulness, then she would have his money. For whatever amount of time we decide to do this, I don't want to be like them. They could've been happy if they fought for their marriage instead of against each other."

He wanted this forever. That confession lived on the tip of Tanner's tongue. He couldn't admit that yet. So he took his wins where he could. "I want to have one of those marriages where we fight for each other. For however long it lasts," Tanner tacked on for Harlan's sake. "We should head upstairs, don't you think?"

Harlan smiled. "Us old married folk need our sleep."

Tanner bit his bottom lip to stop himself from smiling like an idiot. He waited to respond until he thought he could sound a little normal. "Something like that."

Harlan stood. "That's what we'll do, then."

Tanner pushed to his feet and dug out a large tip for the poor woman who had been subjected to listening to their bull-shit while waiting to see if they placed any bets. It was her job. Likely she heard a lot of things in a place like this. She wore a bland smile as he passed the money her way.

"Thanks for your help."

She dipped her chin. Then Harlan's hand was in his as they headed for the elevator. Their bed waited upstairs. It called Tanner's name.

Hot water ran between their bodies. Their tongues slowly played. Something grew in Harlan's chest by the minute. Tanner wanted to be exclusive. To Harlan's surprise, he really wanted that too. The idea of Tanner with someone else had gnawed at him for a while. He hadn't expected to turn possessive of a husband who was supposed to be temporary, but there it was. The jealousy stared him in the face every day, waiting to take him down like a hungry cheetah. He recognized he couldn't ask such a thing of Tanner if he couldn't give the same. For whatever reason, the idea of anyone else touching him made his skin crawl. He was in trouble. This would not end well. Harlan was headed straight for heartbreak at top speed. He couldn't stop.

Tanner's huge body had him engulfed. His arms and hands squeezed and pulled. Their slick bodies moved against each other, as if impatient to become one. Harlan could barely breathe past the lust.

"Goddamn. I don't know what I'll do when summer training begins. You've spoiled me."

Harlan's throat swelled at Tanner's mention of being apart. Maybe it was the desire. Harlan couldn't be sure, but his mouth had things to say his brain hadn't considered. "So come with me."

Tanner went from kissing Harlan's neck to holding his stare. "Do you really want me there?"

Did he? Honestly, at the moment, Harlan didn't want to be apart from Tanner ever again. That was probably his dick, but fuck. He was weak. "Yeah, I want you there."

"And when the season starts, what then?"

Harlan licked his lips. Nervousness set in. This marriage was getting scarily real. "Come with me then too. I know you have your own shit and—"

"No. I can work it out. I'd rather be with you."

Harlan was the middle child all the way to his soul. No one had ever chosen him above every other choice. Tanner did. Harlan's heart was in so much trouble. "Okay."

A huge smile exploded across Tanner's face. "Okay." Tanner's elated expression didn't waver as he dropped to his knees. Harlan's gaze followed. He was hard as stone, with Tanner ready to blow him.

Harlan touched his chin, bringing Tanner's gaze to his. Tanner looked so aroused, Harlan's knees weakened. "You know this is a favor I won't return." Harlan didn't suck dick.

The lust swimming in Tanner's eyes didn't dim. "I'll ride a toy while you watch later."

"Damn. I want that."

Tanner pushed, forcing Harlan against the wall while clinging to his hips. "Then give me what I want." Tanner didn't wait for permission. He took Harlan down his throat. The back of Harlan's head hit the wall. He sucked air. Tanner had an amazing mouth backed by years of experience. Harlan never lasted long with Tanner intent on sucking out his soul. Harlan held Tanner's hair and fucked his face. Everything disappeared except the suction on his cock. The pleasure and pressure grew. He turned more desperate by the second. When the orgasm hit and while he filled Tanner's mouth with cum, the scariest thought of all hit. This was forever. Harlan wouldn't let go without a fight.

CHAPTER SIX

APRIL

Tanner: *I'm headed home. Do you need anything from the store?*

Harlan: *I can't tell you how hilarious it is to me that one of the richest men in the world is running to the store for milk on his way home.*

Tanner: *Milk. Check.*

Harlan: *That was an observation. Not a request.*

Tanner: *Milk. Uncheck.*

May

Harlan: *Matt's birthday is next week. Do you want to go to New Orleans to surprise him?*

Tanner: *Sure. Sounds fun.*

June

Tanner: *These meetings are boring as hell, especially when I want to be home with you.*

Harlan: *Poor baby. I'll be waiting, keeping our bed warm.*

Tanner: *Mhmm. Our bed. I can't wait.*

July

Tanner: *What's your favorite color?*

Harlan: *Why?*

Tanner: **sigh* Just answer the question.*

Harlan: *Red. Now why?*

Tanner: *Oh good. They have a red Bugatti in stock.*

Harlan: *You're not buying me a car.*

Tanner: *No hablo inglés.*

Harlan: *FFS*

August

Harlan: *I'm feeling some sort of way without you home.*

Tanner: *You miss me :-D*

Harlan: *I wouldn't go that far.*

Tanner:

September

Tanner: *The first game of the preseason starts this Tuesday. Want to go?*

Harlan: *I just checked my schedule and I'm free.*

Tanner: *Yay.*

October

Tanner: *Matching costumes? For this Halloween thing Saturday with your team?*

Harlan: **sigh* That's fine.*

Tanner: *Yay!*

November

Tanner couldn't lie and say juggling his life with Harlan wasn't exhausting. While he had great people running his businesses and teams, he still had meetings and whatnot that had him jetting around the world. Harlan had been great. He never expected Tanner to kill himself to make a game. But after eight months of marriage and thriving, Tanner wanted to be as present as possible. He also couldn't claim Harlan wasn't meeting him halfway. Around his schedule, he went back to Canada with him as often as possible. Tanner still lived in fear of one of them breaking under the strain.

He dipped his chin and hid a yawn. These business meetings were killing him. Under the table, while lawyers droned on, Tanner pulled out his phone.

> Tanner: *I hope your practice doesn't last all day.*

To his surprise, his phone buzzed almost immediately with an incoming message.

> Harlan: *It just ended. How about your meeting?*

> Tanner: *Still going.*

> Harlan: *Shouldn't you be paying attention?*

> Tanner: *Probably. I'd rather talk to you.*

> Harlan: *I miss you too.*

A smile exploded across Tanner's face. Silence cut through his joy. He lifted his head. Everyone stared at him, obviously waiting for his attention.

Tanner cleared his throat. "Continue. I'm not paying you to stare at me."

The droning continued, and Tanner tried not to pout. He was thousands of miles from Harlan. These separations didn't happen often. Tanner still hated them. It was already five p.m. There was no way he would make it back to Harlan tonight. He wanted to growl. The meeting crept. It was seven before he finally untangled himself. He burst from the downtown building like the place was on fire. Tanner sucked in a breath of cold Toronto air.

"Mr. Paige?"

The questioning voice had him turning his head. The last person he expected to see stood nearby. Storm eyed him as if every bit as shocked to accidentally run into someone thousands of miles from their last meeting.

"Storm. Hey. It's Tanner, by the way. What an odd surprise."

A huge smile stretched Storm's lips. He looked different tonight. His bottom lip had a piercing in the center and his hair was shaggier than the last time they had met.

"It's good to see you all the same. I hate that I missed our meeting this past summer."

They met in the middle and shook hands. "It's fine. I understand you were injured during the last game of the season. That makes it harder to negotiate. I would've done so all the same. You have a lot of talent."

"I appreciate that." Storm peeked around him. "Where's your husband tonight?"

"He had a mandatory practice in L.A. today. I had a meeting with lawyers I couldn't avoid. It's like that sometimes. What brings you to Toronto?"

"Well, I'm from Pickering. But we play here tomorrow. I came early to enjoy the weather."

They shared a smile. Living hot places didn't always sit well with Canadians. "Where were you headed?"

Storm motioned toward the left with his hand still in his coat pocket. "There's a small pizza place down that way. I always stop there when I'm in town."

Tanner nodded. "Grandpa Tony's Pizza. I eat there a lot. It's my favorite pizza place."

"Right?" Storm's voice filled with happiness. "The first time I stepped in the door and saw an old Italian man tossing dough in the air, I knew it would be good."

They chuckled.

Storm cocked his head to one side and eyed Tanner. "Would you like to join me? I don't mind eating alone. But I also wouldn't mind the company."

Tanner shrugged. He didn't have anything else going on and it would give him the chance to find out what it would take to steal Storm from Vegas. "Sure."

They fell into step beside each other and headed toward the restaurant. "This won't get you in trouble with Harlan, will it?"

The question caught Tanner off guard. "I don't see why it would. It's not like this is a date or anything like that."

Storm nodded. "True. I guess it takes a strong relationship to withstand having careers so far apart. Crazy busy ones at that. Not that I would know," Storm tacked on, sounding sad and distant.

The comment about strength sank into Tanner's blood. They were strong. He spent so much time worrying about the day Harlan would want things to end. It never occurred to him to take a step back and look at them. They were fighting to stay together. This was a real marriage. He didn't know when it had happened. Maybe it had always been real. Either way, they were a genuine couple. Tanner said the one thing he should have been saying to Harlan.

"I love him. He's worth every sacrifice."

Storm flashed him a smile. "That's amazing. It's nice to know that kind of love still exists in the world."

It was amazing. It was also long past the time he should have admitted he wanted this for good. They needed to make some long-term decisions about their future. Tanner still had fears about them burning out and he needed to fix them. He would. Starting tomorrow, they would be permanently married and glued to each other's sides. That was a vow.

The house felt empty as hell without Tanner's larger-than-life presence. Until Harlan had spent his first night without Tanner, he hadn't realized how much space he filled. He was loud and clingy. Tanner was funny and childlike. He was spoiled and pouty when he didn't get his way. Tanner was a constant challenge. Harlan had never loved someone more. He hated these nights alone.

Harlan turned the TV off and on a dozen times. Nothing held his attention. He tapped his phone on his knee, willing Tanner to call. It was likely Tanner was still in his meeting. Harlan didn't want to bug him. The doorbell rang, startling Harlan. No one could make it to his door unless they knew the code to his front gate. At the time of buying the house, he hadn't realized how much he would appreciate that feature until he married Tanner. The media still hadn't let it go. He opened an app on his phone to bring up the front camera. Harlan blinked at the sight of Rider on his porch. He headed for the door.

When Harlan pulled open the door and set eyes on his brother, he realized how much he had missed him. "Hey. You're a long way from home."

Rider smiled. "It's never too far to visit my brother."

Harlan stepped aside. "Come in."

Rider stepped inside and looked around. "Where's Tanner?"

Harlan closed the door as he answered. "He had a meeting with his attorneys tonight and I had mandatory practice. He'll be home tomorrow."

Rider nodded. "That can't be easy."

Harlan smiled in response. He didn't know what to say. Sometimes it was hard as hell, but Harlan couldn't complain. It was his career forcing them apart. Harlan motioned toward the living room. "I was just trying to find something to watch. Do you want something to drink?"

Rider shook his head and claimed a spot on the couch. "Nah. Ben's waiting for me back at the hotel. I brought him out to see your game this Sunday."

That confused Harlan. He reclaimed the recliner he had abandoned to answer the door. "Why didn't you bring him along? You two could've stayed with me."

Rider shrugged. "Honestly, I didn't know if you'd be home. With you constantly going between here and Toronto, I didn't want to complicate things any more. Plus, I hoped to talk to you alone."

Dread rose in Harlan's gut. "Okay. About what?"

After leaning forward and bracing his elbows on his knees, Rider blew out an audible breath. "I need to apologize."

"You really don't."

Rider held up his hand, stopping Harlan. "No. I really do. When I confronted you after the news hit, I didn't handle things well. I've known Tanner for a very long time. When I heard he had married one of my brothers, it nearly sent me over the edge. For as long as I've known Tanner, he's been heartless and a player. He had a different guy every time I saw him. The idea of you marrying someone like our dad was the worst thing I could think to happen to anyone. Much less my little brother. I didn't know how to handle it. Obviously, I did so very badly. But I love you. I always have. There's nothing you could do to make me think badly of you. I was just scared for both of you."

Rider took another audible breath. Before Harlan could thank him for being the bigger person, Rider continued.

"I've seen all the coverage of your marriage. Hell, there's no avoiding it. Every sports channel is like a twenty-four-seven Tanner and Harlan special. What I've seen makes me realize exactly how wrong I was. Every time they show pictures of you two, I can see how much you love each other. I don't know how this came to be or how long it went on underneath my nose, but I'm happy for you. You deserve this."

The swelling in Harlan's throat nearly choked him. He really wished it was true. He fought the urge to confess their marriage wasn't the genuine thing. It was temporary, and that knowledge suffocated him a little more every day. Instead, he chose a different truth to explain his sudden mood shift. "It's not been easy with my career here and his in Canada. Honestly, I live in constant fear he'll get burned out and sick of having to run himself into the ground to make things work. Things never sounded easy, but." Harlan made a gesture, showing he had nothing. The entire situation weighed on him heavier every day.

Rider sat back. He looked thoughtful. "What options have you two considered to make things easier?"

Harlan shrugged.

Rider's eyes filled with laughter. "You two have talked about it, right?"

Discomfort set in. "Not really. We just kind of line up our schedules the best we can."

"Okay." Rider stared into space for a moment, as if working on a puzzle in his mind. Harlan watched in silence. Rider was the smartest and most adult-like person he knew. In his heart, Harlan always believed Rider knew the answer to every question.

Finally, Rider focused on him. "If I ask you right now how to fix it, how would you answer? Tell me the first thing that pops into your head without thinking about it."

"I should retire." Harlan didn't need to consider the question. He had been thinking about it nonstop.

"Is that really what you want?"

Harlan shrugged.

"What do you think Tanner would say about that idea?"

Harlan considered the question, matching it with everything he knew about Tanner. "He'd hate it because he'd think I was giving up everything just for him."

Rider stared at him for a second, as if seeing his soul. "Would you give up everything just for him?"

Harlan didn't hesitate. "Yes." The word popped out so quickly, it resonated with Harlan. He didn't only think he was in love with Tanner. Harlan knew it all the way to his soul. And all the way to his core, Harlan believed Tanner loved him too. Two people didn't work this hard for nothing. Plus, he felt the love. Every time Tanner touched him or even looked at him, Harlan felt cherished. It was doubly obvious to him because no one had ever loved him so unconditionally.

Rider nodded. "Maybe make the suggestion to open the dialogue. Nothing will show him how serious you are, like offering to walk away from a career that other people would kill to have." A smile exploded across Rider's face. "That's exactly how I proved to Ben nothing was more important to me than him."

Harlan nodded. He didn't know how to start that conversation. Each time he thought he could, an unexpected fear rose inside him. What if he only saw a love he wanted to see? What if Tanner was still just waiting for Harlan to let him know when to start untangling their marriage? Maybe Tanner stayed in this marriage out of respect for their friendship. Tanner had lived over fifty years of having a different man every week. How long before Harlan bored him? Maybe he already did.

For several minutes after Tanner left, Storm sat at the table they shared and waited. He knew better than to leave. Like clockwork, the air stirred at his back. Three large figures filled the otherwise empty dining room. One claimed the chair Tanner left behind. He flipped open the jacket of his thirty-thousand-dollar suit as he sat, exposing the gun he wore beneath.

"Did you think no one would call me when you came here with another man?"

Storm fought the urge to play with his lip ring in his nervousness. Barrett stared at him with hard blue eyes, waiting for Storm's response. His gaze moved over

Barrett's light hair—like ice. Cold like the man. "I knew they'd call."

Barrett ran his tongue across his teeth. "So this was some childish ploy to make me jealous?" He sounded so sure. So confident.

"You'd have to care about me to be jealous. We both know that's not the case."

They held each other's stare.

A muscle ticked in Barrett's cut jaw. His sharp angles looked twice as pronounced as he obviously fought not to strike out.

Storm released the breath he held, breaking first the way he always did. "I had dinner with Tanner Paige. He owns the New Orleans Chuckers. He's shown interest in acquiring me from Vegas. That's all."

Barrett's face relaxed, but not by much. "Good. New Orleans is closer than Vegas. As long as you haven't forgotten, you're not free. Your career is the only reason I tolerate this space you've created."

Storm turned his head and stared out the window. How could he forget? Every hour of the day, he knew he wasn't free. He never forgot he was the one who made this choice. Storm had been the biggest of fools to think Barrett might choose him, the way Tanner had chosen Harlan. His life had never been lonelier thanks to that childish dream. It was too bad he still didn't know how to stop.

CHAPTER SEVEN

THE HOUSE WAS EERILY quiet as Tanner came through the door. He had left as early as possible to get back to Harlan. Tanner moved through the house, going from room to room, finding each one empty. Harlan was nowhere to be seen. All their cars were in the garage. An odd sort of panic came from left field and sideswiped him. He couldn't explain it. There was just a horrible feeling in his gut.

Finally, he noticed the French doors leading to their bedroom balcony were slightly ajar. He peeked out. Harlan sat on the balcony with his feet resting on the railing. He stared at nothing.

Tanner stepped outside.

Harlan's head turned. A sweet, if not tired-looking smile touched his lips. "Hey, baby. I didn't know when you'd be home."

Tanner bent and stole a kiss. "Sorry. I should've texted you on my way. With the time difference, I didn't want to wake you."

Harlan snagged his t-shirt before he got away and stole another kiss.

As always, he couldn't stop smiling. Despite Harlan's amazing greeting, he wasn't smiling. "What's wrong?"

"We need to talk about our marriage."

Tanner sat. Thankfully, there was a chair to catch him, because Tanner's knees simply wouldn't hold him any longer. "Oh. Okay."

Harlan's gaze moved over Tanner's face as if searching for something. "Rider says you used to have a different man every time he saw you. Am I keeping you from that?" He didn't give Tanner time to answer. "Am I exhausting you to the point you'll hate me eventually?"

Tanner knew his expression had to match his level of confusion. "When did Rider say that? Where's all this coming from?"

A sad smile touched Harlan's lips. "I've been thinking about it for a while. Honestly, things have been so great, I haven't considered maybe you're ready to untangle this. It's possible I'm stealing your life all because I can't let my brother be right."

The pains in Tanner's chest grew, making it harder for him to breathe. "Is that why you haven't asked for a divorce yet? Is being with me all about your brother?"

Harlan swallowed. It looked painful. "No. That's not why."

"Then why?"

Harlan looked away. "You didn't answer me. I guess that means I was right to worry. You can ask your lawyers to untangle this marriage. I won't keep you hopping planes and wasting time any longer."

Tanner thought his chest might explode. The pain was too big. "What if that's not what I want?"

Harlan met his stare again.

Tanner's pulse sounded loud in his ears. "I walked through the door, excited to tell you about a plan I have to keep me from having to go back home when you need to be here. Now you want a divorce."

"I don't want a divorce."

They stared at each other. Harlan sounded sad, and Tanner didn't understand.

"Then why are we having this conversation?"

Harlan swallowed again. "Because I love you and I don't want to burn you out or make you hate me. I want you to be happy, even if that means you won't be with me."

Honestly, Tanner didn't hear a word past Harlan admitting he loved him. Tanner stood and had Harlan over his shoulder in an instant. A surprised-sounding yelp escaped Harlan, but he didn't fight. Tanner carried him inside and tossed him on the bed. Before Harlan rallied, Tanner straddled him, pinning him to the bed.

"Don't ever talk about divorcing me again."

Harlan blinked. "Okay."

Tanner gave him a sharp nod. "I have something to say."

Harlan looked more confused by the moment. "All right."

There was no going back. "I was stone cold sober when I married you." Harlan's lips parted in surprise. Tanner kept going before Harlan could run. "Since we met at Rider's party, I've never been more obsessed. Before that day, it is possible I had a different man every time Rider saw me. That's because I wasn't happy. I didn't want an unhappy relationship like my parents had, so I couldn't stop searching for something different. Everyone I met made me feel like... I don't know. I can't explain it. Like, I'm unbothered by someone using me for my money. That's to be expected, but it was like everyone I met was fake. They were just pretending to be what they thought I wanted. You never did that. From day one, you made it clear you only spent time with me because you want to and wouldn't the moment you didn't want to anymore. But we clicked."

Tanner knew he wasn't explaining himself well, but he was trying. "Then we walked past that twenty-four-hour wedding chapel. You looked at me and said, 'No one will ever want to marry me. I'm too selfish.' And I said, 'I will. I'll marry you.' The next thing I knew, I was pulling every string and cashing in every favor to marry you before you changed your mind. It never occurred to me you wouldn't remember. But then you didn't, and I couldn't lose you, so I just did whatever you needed me to do to keep you. I might've agreed to stay married because you asked. But really, I've never wanted anything more than I do this marriage. I love you. How can you be so blind you don't see that?"

Harlan sniffed, nearly breaking Tanner. Harlan was too strong and independent to be on the verge of tears. Yet Tanner watched it happen. "I think this should be my last season with the team."

Of all the things Harlan could've chosen to say, that one confused him the most. "Why? Where did that come from?"

Harlan sniffed again. "I just want to be with you, and all this back and forth is just too hard. This bed was so fucking empty last night. I don't want to feel like that anymore."

As much as Tanner wanted to smile at the confession, he didn't think he should. "Baby, I would never expect you to give up the career you love. I actually came up with a plan. Well, Storm did."

A line appeared between Harlan's eyebrows. "Storm?"

Tanner nodded. He rolled to his side. With his head propped up on his hand, he kept one leg across Harlan's body. "Yeah. As I was leaving my meeting last night, I ran into him on the street. Apparently, Vegas is playing in Toronto today. Anyhow, he asked about you, and I explained how our schedules sometimes collide and I have to be there while you're here. He suggested I hire a company to set up a high-security virtual office to hold meetings, so I don't have to leave you. I didn't know that was a thing, which really just proves I'm getting old. Technology is out-pacing me. But anyway, I think that's a great idea. I could have my meetings online and never miss a night with you."

"Wow." Harlan blinked. "That's... wow. I guess I kind of knew that was a thing with more people working from home and whatnot, but I assumed you had to be physically present to sign things and whatnot."

"Nope. I can do that virtually as well."

Harlan stared at the ceiling. "Damn." A smile played on his lips. "We might really get to have a normal marriage."

Tanner shrugged. "Well, as normal as you and I will ever be. Would you really quit football just to be with me?"

Harlan met his stare. Those gorgeous light blue eyes stole Tanner's heart the way they always did. "I'm a little scared of how far I would go to stay with you." His expression turned guilty. "The day I woke up and realized we were married, everything came back to me after a hot shower. I didn't say anything because I didn't realize you had been sober. We had a lot to drink that night. I didn't want to be the only one who remembered we had jumped into this marriage with both feet completely and willingly."

Tanner's face hurt from smiling. "I'm a big guy. If there's one thing I do well, it's hold my liquor."

Harlan swiped a hand over his eyes. He snorted. "What the fuck is wrong with us?"

"Do you want a list?"

A laugh burst from Harlan. "Not really, no. I might need therapy otherwise."

Tanner kissed Harlan's cheek. "I'll do therapy with you." He kissed Harlan's ear.

"I'll do anything if you'll tell me you love me again."

"Anything?" Harlan's breathless tone had Tanner's dick stirring.

"Mmm. Anything." Tanner nibbled his way down Harlan's neck.

"I love you."

Tanner's eyes unexpectedly burned. "I love you too. It would kill me if you decided you didn't want this anymore."

In a flash, Harlan had Tanner on his back. He straddled him. "Never." Harlan's mouth covered his. Their tongues fought. Every lick had Tanner getting hotter by the second. Harlan tugged at his clothes, stripping Tanner between kisses. Once he had Tanner nude, Harlan shocked him speechless by licking his cock from root to tip. Tanner went still, afraid to move in case Harlan changed his mind. Harlan had dated more women than men. He was a hardcore top and did not suck dick. That wasn't something Tanner cared about. He didn't need that in his life. He would rather have Harlan. But if Harlan wanted to do something new with him, Tanner was there for it.

Still, he felt the need to reassure Harlan. "You don't have to. I love you the way you are."

Harlan didn't respond. He didn't acknowledge Tanner's words at all. His mouth closed around the tip of Tanner's erection. Tanner couldn't control the moan that escaped him. The sound obviously emboldened him. Harlan took him a little deeper.

"Holy shit. You're killing me." Because it was Harlan, and there was no one sexier in Tanner's eyes. Another sound he couldn't swallow vibrated from his throat.

Harlan shot to his knees. "I'm sorry. Maybe some other time, but I can't take it. The sounds you're making are killing me." Harlan scrambled for the lube. In seconds, he impaled Tanner. They froze. Harlan held his stare. He rocked, as if silently asking for permission to keep going.

Tanner snagged the back of Harlan's neck and claimed his mouth. He did the best he could to use Harlan's dick.

Finally, Harlan got the message. He sawed in and out, taking Tanner's ass hard. Tanner was on cloud nine. Every second was more amazing than the last. Harlan loved him. They would stay married. Nothing else mattered in the entire world.

There was nothing Harlan wouldn't do to please Tanner. Unfortunately, he had zero patience left. Tanner had admitted to loving him. He wanted this marriage. Harlan had to seal the deal with an orgasm. Harlan needed Tanner to know he never needed to go elsewhere. He had everything Tanner would ever want.

Unfortunately, Tanner made him too hot. Harlan had zero patience. He had to feel

Tanner orgasming around his dick. Harlan had to feel that heat milking him.

"Come for me. I want to pump you full of cum and watch you leak."

"Oh god."

Tanner sounded like he could barely breathe. That was exactly where Harlan wanted him.

"That's it, baby. You look so sexy wearing my dick. Give me everything."

"I love you so much."

His heart and mind had been completely stolen. Now he wanted Tanner to take his soul too. "I love you too, gorgeous. Blow for me. Let me watch."

A whine came from the back of Tanner's throat. His body tensed. Harlan held his breath. When Tanner's body jerked, Harlan sucked in a sharp breath. The pleasure was too much. Between watching cum squirt from Tanner and the sensation of his asshole tightening around him sent him over the edge. Harlan cried out as he pumped cum inside Tanner, filling his ass. It was one of the hottest moments of his life—like a claiming. He savored every blast of ecstasy until the feeling ebbed, leaving behind only euphoria. Harlan kissed Tanner, indulging in the freedom to love him without fear or hiding. He didn't have to hope Tanner didn't see the love in his eyes and run. Everything was out there now. This was real. They were truly until death did they part. It was wild and exhilarating. Tanner had a way of keeping him high. All the partying and bed hopping of his past didn't compare to the thrill this one man brought to his life. Tanner was the only ride through life Harlan would ever need again. He was Harlan's heart. His everything.

CHAPTER EIGHT

THE CROWD SEEMED EXTRA loud today. Harlan's head pounded. The sun was at that perfect angle to blind him, no matter which way he looked. He bounced on his toes and paced the sidelines. Occasionally, he practiced his kick, keeping warm for the next field goal. They were up by twenty-one and the other team kept resorting to playing dirty. It was always like this when they played their rival

Northern California team. The bad blood between them was notorious.

"Call from the box."

Harlan's gaze shot to the sideline manager. No one ever called him from the owner's box. With a nod, he accepted the device. He pressed it to his ear.

"Your ass looks amazing in those pants. Why don't you wear them for me at home?"

Harlan's mood lifted. He turned his face toward the box. From his position, he couldn't see Tanner, but he knew he was there watching. With a chuckle, Harlan handed the device back without responding. He couldn't stop smiling.

"Get ready. One more solid push and we'll be in field goal range."

Harlan nodded. He didn't usually need to be warned, but Tanner had him distracted. Harlan moved back to the practice net and jogged toward it before kicking out, keeping his hamstring stretched and ready to go. His nerves never eased. Not even after a decade. His job was a huge part of whether they won or lost. A missed field goal could make all the difference. If he failed, it might be the only thing talked about on all the sports channels for the next week. He hopped, getting his blood pumping. It was almost his time. He had to pound the final nail in this coffin so he could go home. Harlan had a husband waiting.

Tanner leaned against the window and eyed Harlan. He looked pumped and sexy. Watching from the owner's box had become a regular thing since they married. The Apollos' team's owner, Billy Freeman, had no qualms about sharing his space. Billy's husband, Neo, was a six-foot-five blond bombshell who spent every game curled up in his husband's lap alongside another player's husband, Omri. Today, Rider and Ben joined them. Tanner enjoyed their company, but Harlan was about to go on the field. Tanner had to be as close to the glass as possible. He had to watch his man in action. Plus, as much as he hated to admit it, he was still kind of pissed off about Rider telling

Harlan he had a different man every time he saw him. He knew Rider only wanted to protect his brother, but Tanner didn't need anything else undermining his marriage. They needed time to grow strong.

The players lined up on the field with Harlan getting into position. Tanner leaned closer to the glass. Harlan ran toward the ball. He kicked. A defenseman jumped the line and collided with Harlan. Harlan went down beneath his opponent and another teammate. A fight ensued over the dirty hit. Tanner bounced in place, needing to see what happened to Harlan.

Harlan didn't get up.

Tanner panicked as someone motioned for help. "I have to get down there."

Billy stood at his back. He squeezed Tanner's shoulders. "Just give it a minute. Let them look at him. Players bounce back up from ugly-looking plays all the time."

"It's true," a deep French accent agreed behind him. "My Tripp goes down all the time. It's very nerve-wracking, but it's part of things. They train for these things."

Tanner held his breath. He wished he could take Omri's claims to heart, but he could see Harlan's face. He was awake but writhing in pain. His panic grew to a fever pitch when several nearby players went down on one knee. That couldn't be good. They were close enough to hear what was being said. Tanner wasn't. Finally, the coach looked around and gave some signal to the sidelines.

"Okay. You need to get down there. They're signaling for an emergency." Billy headed for the door. Tanner was hot on his heels, followed closely by Rider and Ben. Billy pulled out his phone. He hit one button and pressed the device to his ear. "Tell me."

Tanner stared hard at Billy, waiting to hear what he learned.

"Okay. I'm headed down there right now with his husband." Billy put his phone away. He glanced over his shoulder. "He has a compound fracture in his right leg. There's always an ambulance on standby for these things. We'll meet them at the left gate, and you can ride with him."

Tanner nodded along. He couldn't breathe. Compound fractures were dangerous. They could pierce important veins and whatnot. His baby was in pain. Tanner needed to get to him.

"We'll meet you at the hospital."

Tanner nodded at Rider's words, but he didn't really hear a thing. The elevator moved too slowly. Tanner was ready to crawl out of his skin. He needed to be with Harlan. Everything felt numb. They reached the left gate as the ambulance pulled through to drive onto the field.

Billy waved them down. "Take him with you."

They slowed long enough for Tanner to jump into the back. He was too numb to even thank Billy for his help. His impatience and the serious expressions of the paramedics had his blood pressure through the roof. It probably didn't take long for them to make it onto the field, but it felt like forever. Finally, the ambulance slowed. He had to force himself to stay seated and not get in the way as the paramedics jumped from the vehicle and pulled out the gurney. Tanner stared so hard at Harlan, looking for any signs of life. He heard him cry out as they moved him onto the gurney. Tanner's heart twisted. He thought he might be sick. It took forever for them to get Harlan ready for transport. Tanner was ready to scream by the time the gurney headed his way.

Finally, Harlan was wheeled in next to him. His eyes were filled with pain. The moment he spotted Tanner, he reached for him. Tanner fought back a wave of tears as the relief of holding his hand hit him.

"I've got you, baby."

Harlan didn't speak. His jaw worked as if he fought a scream. But he squeezed Tanner's hand, as if drawing on Tanner's strength. That was enough. Tanner wasn't going anywhere.

Everything spun. Harlan had never been given so many painkillers at one time in his life. Between whatever they shot him up with on the field, surgery, and then whatever they had in a bag taped to his skin to wear home, he felt nothing. But his head spun, and the room spun, making him sick to his stomach. He kept his eyes squeezed shut as Tanner carried him through the door.

"Come on. Let's get you tucked into bed so you can finally sleep."

He hoped once Tanner put him to bed, he would feel less nauseous. Unfortunately, the moment he was flat on his back, the room spun faster. He clutched his head. "Goddamn. Please make it stop. I don't want to get sick."

Tanner looked so worried. Harlan felt guilty for begging. He just felt so fucking bad, and there was no way he could run to the bathroom to puke.

"It's all right, baby. I've got you." Tanner sat him up and then climbed in behind him, so Harlan reclined between Tanner's legs with his head on Tanner's chest. Once he got them settled, he pulled the blankets over them. He held

Harlan so tightly, it grounded him. Things slowed around him. His stomach settled.

"Oh, thank god. Thank you."

Tanner kissed his temple. "You never have to thank me. I'll accept any excuse to hold you." He paused. "Except maybe don't do this again. I've never been so scared in my life."

"Don't worry. I'm done."

"You're definitely out for the season. This'll take time to heal."

Harlan shook his head. He regretted it almost immediately. It took a few seconds of swallowing bile before he could respond. "No. I'm done for good."

"You can recover from this. There's no need to give up already."

Harlan made a wild gesture he couldn't control, as high as he was. "No. I've been thinking about it for a while. Even with this new virtual office, we'll still be running ourselves into an early grave. I just want to be with you. This career has been good to me. I don't want to go out being mediocre. I just want to sit like this with you. Maybe a little less injured, but you know what I mean. Let's just slow down."

Tanner pressed his lips to the shell of Harlan's ear and stayed there, soothing him with the sound of his breathing. He spoke quietly. "When you have a little less drugs in you, we'll figure things out. For now, just rest. I'll be right here, holding you."

When Harlan responded, he sounded half asleep, even to his ears. It was out of his control. "The day I met you, I thought you were a spoiled asshole who wasn't used to hearing no." He felt Tanner smile against his ear. Harlan kept going. "Luckily, I find that hot since you're all those things and the best thing that's ever happened to me."

Tanner chuckled. It was a low and sexy sound. A smile pulled at Harlan's lips and his eyes fell closed as Tanner began to softly sing against his ear. It was the same love song that played when they had shared the first slow dance. His muscles relaxed. Every day, something else happened that let him know he had made the best choice of his life when he married Tanner. He could sleep and everything would be okay. Soon, they would move to Canada permanently and move at a slower pace. He couldn't wait to be held like this all the time, with a lot less pain involved.

"I brought Harlan's stuff from the arena and Ben drove your car home. It's in the garage."

Tanner stopped singing at Rider's arrival. Harlan couldn't open his eyes. He didn't know if he was more asleep than awake, but he was completely relaxed and at peace for once. He didn't want to move and risk sending the room spinning again. So he simply listened to Rider and Tanner's conversation.

"Thank you. I'm lucky you two were here to help."

Silence met Tanner's claim. After a moment, Rider cleared his throat. "I owe you an apology. When I first learned you'd married my brother, I was furious.

I thought this was just another game for you." Rider cleared his throat again. "But it's obvious I was wrong, and you really love my brother. Thank you for that. He needs that, and he deserves it."

Another sweet kiss brushed Harlan's ear. "You never have to thank me for this. He wasn't the only one of us who needed this marriage."

Rider's voice turned businesslike. "Well, Ben and I have to head back home. We need to be ready for Tuesday's home game. If you two need anything, we're just a phone call away. When Harlan wakes up, please tell him to call me and keep me updated."

"I will. Be careful going home."

A few moments passed. Harlan thought maybe he dozed.

Tanner chuckled. "Call your brother and keep him updated."

Harlan smiled. "How did you know I'm still awake?"

Tanner's arms tightened around him. "I know everything about you, especially how you sound when you're sleeping. I've spent a lot of nights awake, watching you sleep and silently begging you to love me the way I love you."

Harlan forced his eyes open. He tilted his head so he could meet Tanner's stare. "You never had to beg. I've always loved you." He closed his eyes again. The exhaustion was winning. "You're the best drunken mistake I've ever made."

He felt Tanner's body shake with laughter. "I'll never let you regret it."

Harlan knew. He didn't need reassur-ances. There were two things in this world Harlan couldn't avoid: death and Tanner's love. He hoped he got years and years of the latter before the former took him. Without a doubt, they would never let each other down.

Keep an eye out for the next Thin Ice, *Pucking Mobbed*.

About the Author

CHARITY PARKERSON IS AN award-winning and multi-published author with several companies. Born with no filter from her brain to her mouth, she decided to take this odd quirk and insert it in her characters. One of her greatest loves is writing morally gray characters. You'll find them scattered throughout her hundreds of titles.

*Eight-time Readers' Favorite Award Winner

*2015 Passionate Plume Award Finalist

*2013 Reviewers' Choice Award Winner

*2012 ARRA Finalist for Favorite Paranormal Romance

*Five-time winner of The Mistress of the Darkpath

Connect with her online:

*Sign up for her newsletter: https://sendfox.com/charityparkerson

*Join her readers' group on Facebook: http://bit.ly/CharitysTribe

*Website: https://www.charityparkerson.com

*A list of her social media accounts and giveaways all in one place: http://hy.page/charityparkerson